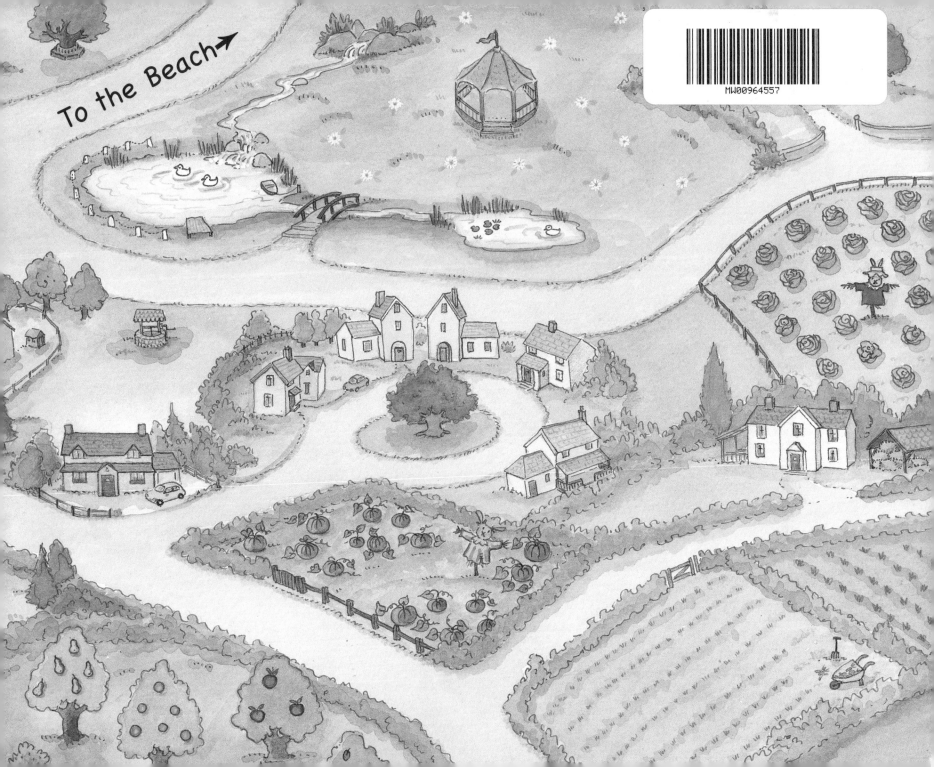

To the Beach→

For Mom, with all my heart.
—MB

For Bessie, Bunty, and Blue, my own sunny bunnies.
—JG

Sunny Bunnies
Text copyright © 2008 by Margie Blumberg/MB Publishing, LLC
Illustrations copyright © 2008 by June Goulding
Book design copyright © 2008 by PageWave Graphics

First published in the United States by MB Publishing, LLC
www.mbpublishing.com
First Edition
10 9 8 7 6 5 4 3 2 1

Library of Congress Control Number: 2008900789
Blumberg, Margie
Sunny Bunnies/by Margie Blumberg; illustrations by June Goulding
p. cm.
Summary: Cheerful illustrations and endearing rhymes reveal a wonderful day
at the beach in Carrot Cake Park for this sister and brother.

ISBN: 978-0-9624166-4-4
Printed in Canada by Friesens

Sunny Bunnies

Written by
Margie Blumberg

Illustrated by
June Goulding

MB PUBLISHING, LLC

We're going to the beach today.
Sun and fun and games to play!
Here's a list of
What we'll do.
Are you ready?
Good! Me, too!

Inch by inch and
Bit by bit.
Somehow they will
Make it fit!

Almost there now—
Smell the sea?

Fling your flip-flops!
Follow me.

Racing pipers,
Fudgey treat,
Striped umbrellas—
Life is sweet!

One wave,
   two waves...

Whoosh-another!

You're all wet now,
Little brother!

Friends to lend a
Helping hand—

That's what makes our
Castle grand!

Lunchtime,
Munchtime,
Yum, yum, yum!

Cake and fruit juice,
Here we come!

Feel it flutter?
Hold on tight!

It takes two to
Fly our kite.

Tag—she caught you!
Stop and freeze.

Drip, drop, plop—Oops!
One more, please.

Pink and purple,
Gold and blue!

We have one more
Thing to do...

Don't you love this roaring fire?
Hear it crackle? See it spark?
It's so warm and bright and cozy—
Keeps us toasty in the dark.

Stars are twinkling,
Say good night...

Up above,
The moon shines bright...

Time for bed—
Sweet dreams, sleep tight.

Aren't you sleepy?

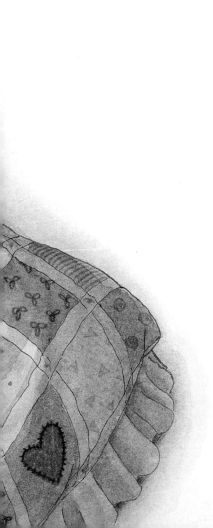

Oh . . .

All right!

Carrot Cake Park

Bunny Hill

Village shops

Carrot Tops School